Salad Pie

written by
Wendy BooydeGraaff

illustrated by
Bryan Langdo

Ripple Grove
Press

To Madeira, for her inspiration,
Ava, for her imagination, and
Stella, for her illumination
— W. B.

For Harper, for all the inspiration
you provide
— B. L.

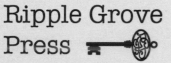

Ripple Grove
Press
Portland, OR
www.RippleGrovePress.com

Text copyright © 2016 by Wendy BooydeGraaff
Illustrations copyright © 2016 by Bryan Langdo

First Edition 2016
Library of Congress Control Number 2015950802
ISBN 978-0-9913866-4-2

10 9 8 7 6 5 4 3 2 1
Printed in South Korea by PACOM

This book was typeset in Gurmukhi MN.
The illustrations were rendered in watercolor on Fabriano paper.
Book design by Amanda Broder

When Maggie arrived at the park, it was empty
and it was quiet.
She smiled. Everything was perfect for making Salad Pie.

Then Herbert appeared.
The park was no longer empty.

"Hi," said Herbert.
The park was no longer quiet.

"What are you doing?" asked Herbert.
The park was no longer perfect.

"I'm working. Working hard," Maggie grumbled.

"I'm making salad. Salad Pie.
And don't you touch it!"

Maggie walked in a wide arc around
Herbert, collecting the
essential ingredients:
five stems of sweetly scented clover,
six squishy crab apples,
three prickly dandelion leaves,

and a shiny, crinkly gum wrapper.

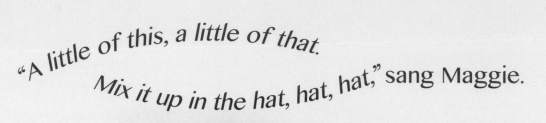

"A little of this, a little of that.

Mix it up in the hat, hat, hat," sang Maggie.

Herbert brought six more stems of clover.
"No thanks, Herbert," said Maggie. "I have enough."

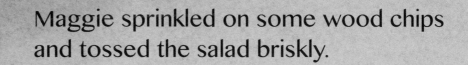

Maggie sprinkled on some wood chips
and tossed the salad briskly.

A few pieces flew out of the hat.

Herbert scurried to pick them up.

Stretching his hand out to Maggie, he almost touched Salad Pie.

Maggie froze.

Gritting her teeth, she growled. "Don't touch!"

Then she took Herbert's wrist and she pulled and stretched until his hand hovered over the salad.

The pieces slid into the hat.

Maggie let go, and Herbert's hand sprang back to his side.

"Magnificent. Very, very magnificent," she said.

Maggie nodded to herself—checking to see if Herbert was watching—and began to dance a jig.

She sang, "Salad Pie, oh Salad Pie!

Soon you'll be ready, Salad Pie."

Tap, tap, tap. Herbert's toes tapped to the beat.

Maggie stopped.
Maggie glared.

Herbert stopped tapping.

Maggie climbed up, up, up, **up** the slide.

"I need to bake it before it can be Salad Pie for real," she said, looking over her shoulder.

"Into the oven," said Maggie, and she closed the imaginary oven door with panache.

Gently, ever so gently, Maggie danced her jig.

Softly, ever so softly, she sang, "Salad Pie, oh Salad Pie!

Soon you'll be ready, Salad Pie."

But Salad Pie wasn't ready, so Maggie danced more and sang more.

She couldn't wait to have that magnificent pie!

Faster and faster, she danced her dance.

Louder and louder, she sang her song.

"Salad Pie, oh Salad Pie!

Soon you'll be ready—"

Salad Pie zoomed rumble-tumble down.

Maggie hurtled pell-mell down.

They bumped and jostled in a jumble

down,
      down,
            down . . .

and Herbert caught them both.

Maggie brushed off her knees and inspected Salad Pie.
It was perfect.
"Let's bake Salad Pie down here," she said.
"Sure," said Herbert.

Maggie tossed the salad one more time. Herbert added more clover and a curved twig on top.

"Nice garnish," said Maggie.

Together, Maggie and Herbert began to dance,
but not too wildly.

Together, they began to sing, but not too loudly.

"Salad Pie, oh Salad Pie!

Soon you'll be ready, Salad Pie."

And together Maggie and Herbert sat down.
They pretended to eat the clover.
They pretended to eat the wood chips
and the curved twig.

They even pretended to eat the shiny gum wrapper.

"It's very magnificent," Herbert said. "It would be even more magnificent with Sandwich Stew!"

Softly, ever so softly, Maggie began to sing.

"Sandwich Stew, oh Sandwich Stew.

Tomorrow we will brew Sandwich Stew."